I'm Bad!

KATE & JIM McMULLAN

JOANNA COTLER BOOKS
An Imprint of HarperCollinsPublishers

Library of Congress Cataloging-in-Publication Data is available.
ISBN 978-0-06-122971-8 (trade bdg.) — ISBN 978-0-06-122972-5 (lib. bdg.)

Typography by Neil Swaab   1 2 3 4 5 6 7 8 9 10   ❖   First Edition

For T. McGhee Louise Steiner

Thanks to the jawsome talents at HarperCollins, Joanna Cotlerex, Karen Nagelosaurus, Alyson Dayodon, Neil Swaabatops, Jaime Morrellimus, Ruiko Tokunagastega, and Kathryn Silsandoceras, and to our kick-a-whomper Pippins, Holly McGheeotitan, Emily van Beekaraptor, Samantha Cosentinotaurus, and Cleo.

Tons of thanks to Dr. Matthew Lamanna, Assistant Curator of Vertebrate Paleontology, Carnegie Museum of Natural History, for his knowledge and his sense of humor.

Are you BAD?

I'm REALLY bad.

Scare-the-tails-off-
all-the-other-dinosaurs

BAD.

Got rip-'em-up CLAWS.

Got bite-'em-up FANGS.

Bad breath?

Yeaaahhhhhhhh

Got a **SWIVEL NECK** for watchin' my back.

Got broad-jump **LEGS** and triple-digit, kick-a-whomper **STOMPERS.**

Did you just call me **BABY ARMS?**

Long as yours, pal—
20 times stronger.
Think about it. . . .

Are you BIG?

I'm REALLY BIG.

6-tons-of-MUSCLE-on the-hustle BIG.
And my BIG empty belly is
growling for GRUB.

rrrrumble

Watch me catch some **TWEETS**.

Aw, who likes feathers anyway?

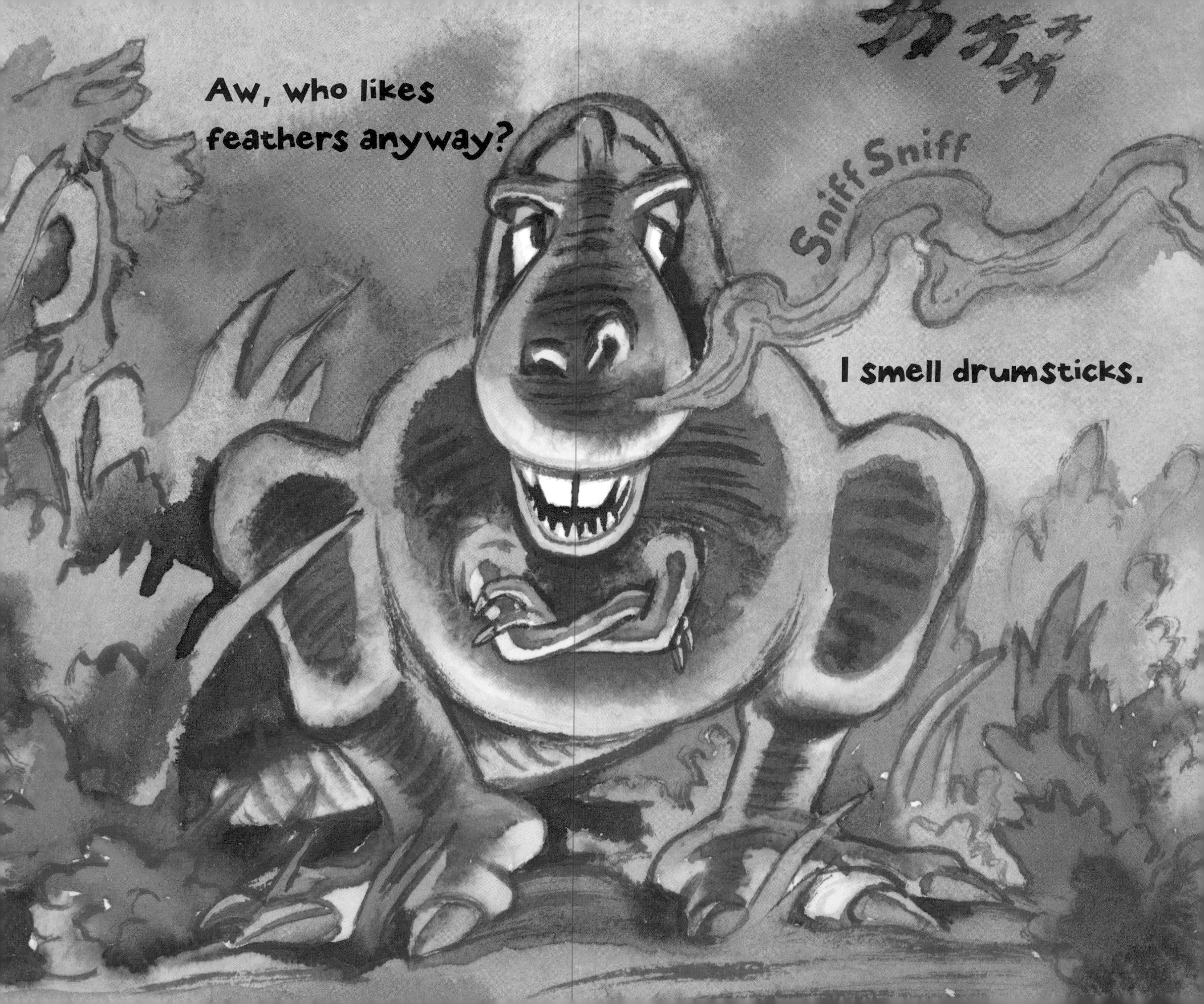

I smell drumsticks.

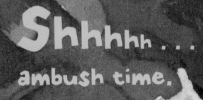

Yer not too **SMALLS**
to be my **MEATBALLS**.

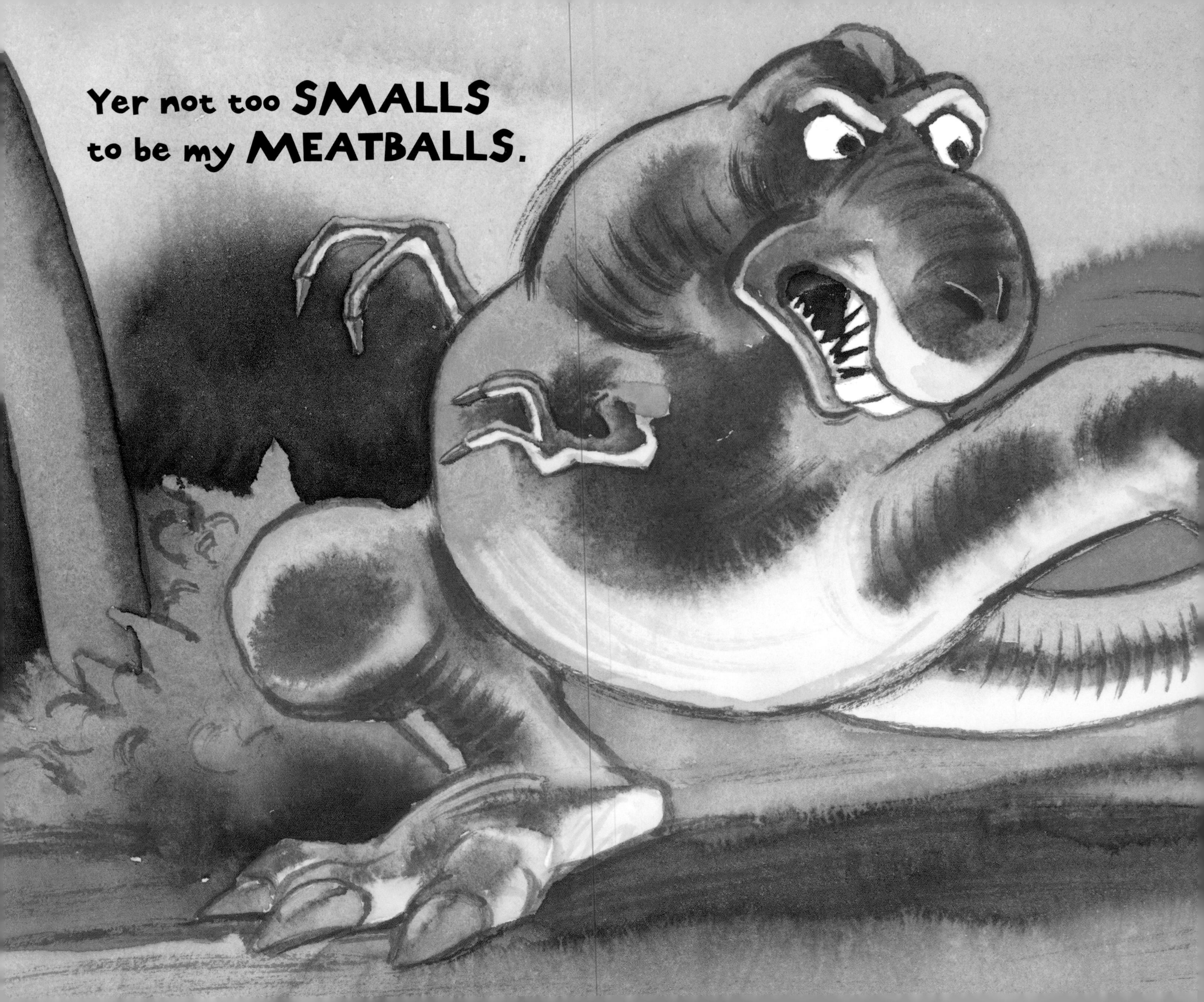

Forget you, fuzzballs.
I got my peepers on a bigger burger.

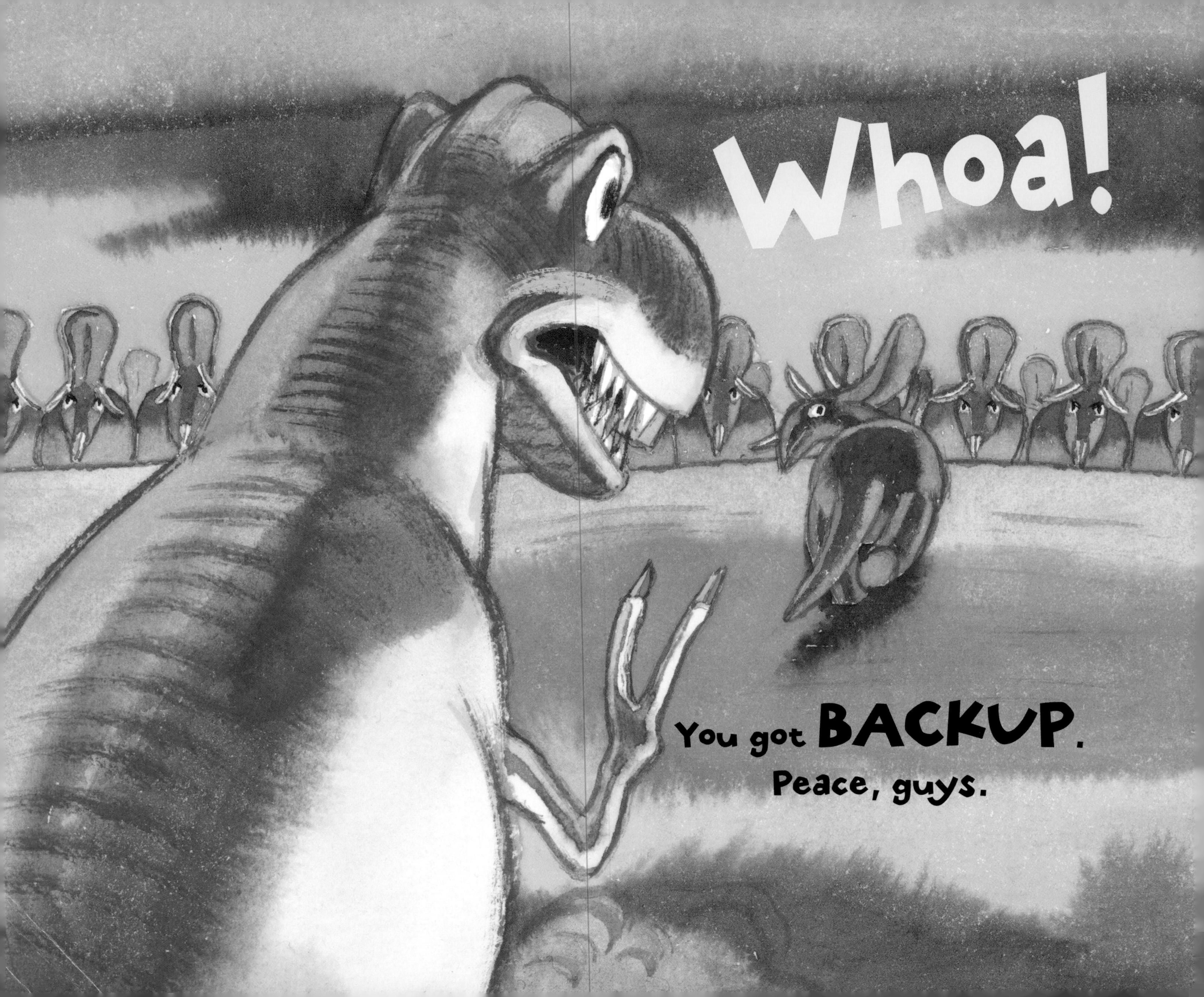

Whoa!

You got **BACKUP**.

Peace, guys.

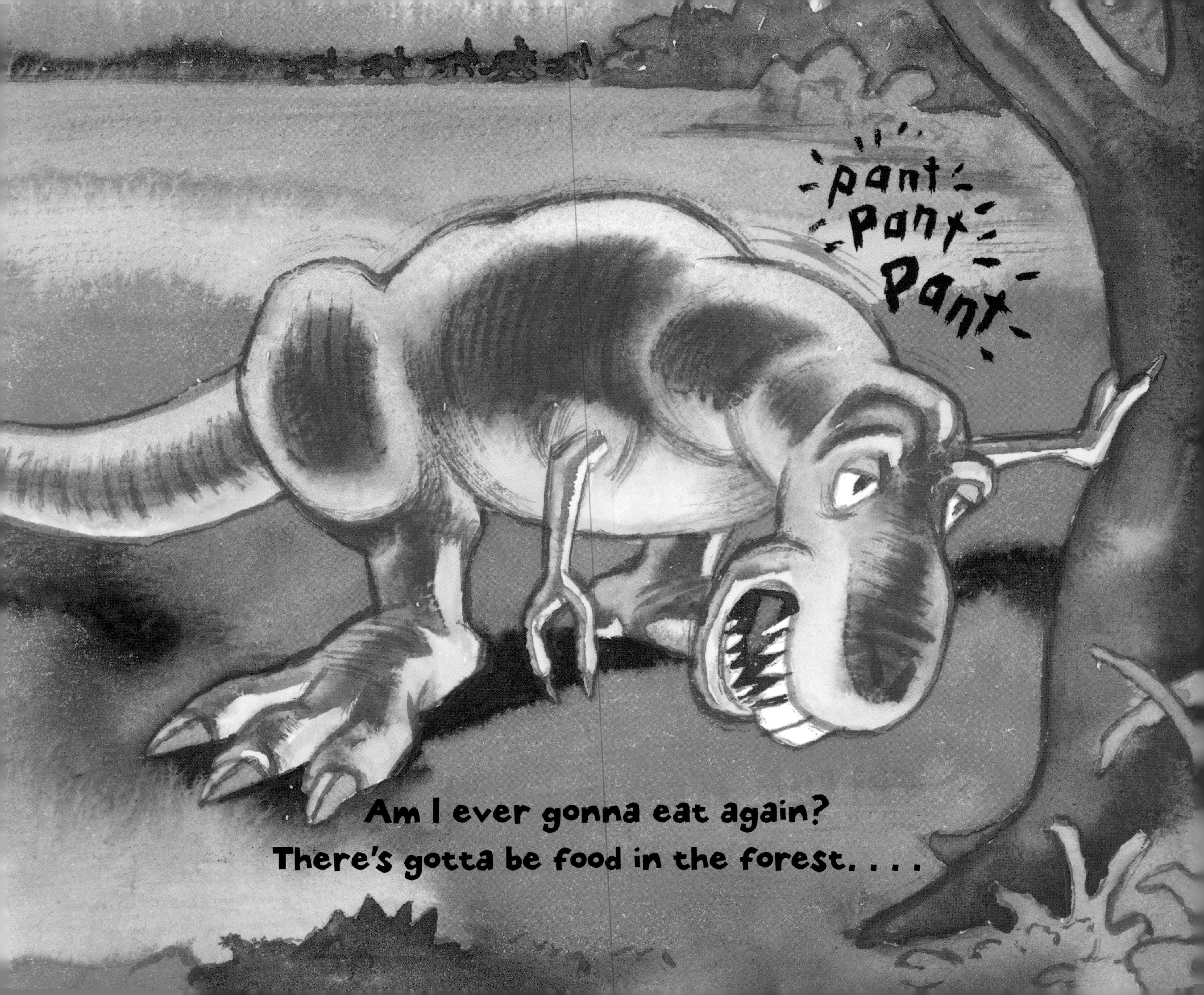

Am I ever gonna eat again?
There's gotta be food in the forest. . . .

I love my mom.

Triceratops

Stygimoloch

Ornithomimus

Pachycephalosaurus